THE LEGEND OF

NINJA
COWBOY
BEAR

THE LEGEND OF
NINJA
COWBOY
BEAR

David Bruins and Hilary Leung

Kids Can Press

For Neuman and Edie — D.B.

For Mom and Dad — H.L.

Once upon a time there were three friends:
a ninja, a cowboy and a bear.

They did everything together and enjoyed each other's company.

However, they were each different in their own way.

One day those differences came between them, and here is what happened.

The ninja and the bear started to quarrel. The ninja thought he was better than the bear. The bear disagreed.

So they asked the cowboy to decide who was better. Unable to choose between his friends, the cowboy arranged a competition to see who could build the largest pile of rocks.

Although the ninja tried his best, in the end his pile was much smaller than the bear's. So the bear boasted that he was unbeatable.

The cowboy disagreed. He thought he could
beat the bear, and they began to argue.

So they asked the ninja to decide who was better. Unable to choose between his friends, the ninja created a competition to see who could pick the most raspberries.

Although the bear tried his best, he could not collect nearly as many raspberries as the cowboy. So the cowboy claimed that no one could beat him.

The ninja disagreed, and another argument began.

So they asked the bear to decide who was better. Unable to choose between his friends, the bear created a competition to see who could catch the most rabbits.

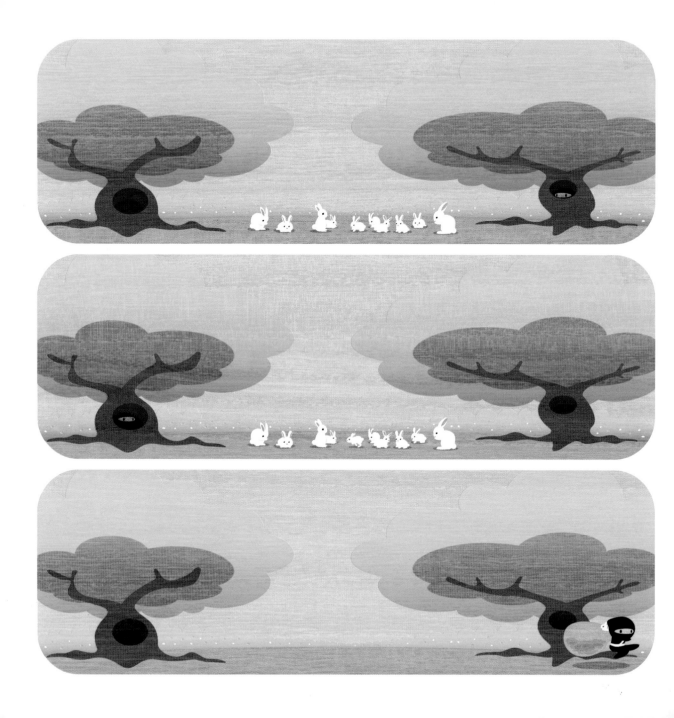

Although the cowboy tried his best,
he could not catch as many rabbits as the ninja.

Afterwards, the three friends were confused. They still did not know who was the best.

Frustrated, they parted ways.

The ninja spent time in quiet meditation.

The bear consulted with a wise old friend.

And the cowboy took to the hills.

And soon, they each realized something very important.

The bear wondered at
the cowboy's precision
and accuracy.

The ninja appreciated
the bear's great strength.

The cowboy was in
awe of the ninja's agility.

The ninja, the cowboy and the bear recognized that
no one had to be the best. They were each special and unique—
just like you and me.

NINJA
BEATS
COWBOY

COWBOY
BEATS
BEAR

BEAR
BEATS
NINJA

Kids Can Press acknowledges the financial support of the Government of Ontario, through the Ontario Media Development Corporation's Ontario Book Initiative; the Ontario Arts Council; the Canada Council for the Arts; and the Government of Canada, through the BPIDP, for our publishing activity.

Published in Canada by
Kids Can Press Ltd.
29 Birch Avenue
Toronto, ON M4V 1E2

Published in the U.S. by
Kids Can Press Ltd.
2250 Military Road
Tonawanda, NY 14150

www.kidscanpress.com

Printed and bound in Singapore

This book is smyth sewn casebound.

CM 09 0 9 8 7 6 5 4 3 2 1

The Japanese characters on page 15 are prounced "Taru ni ki-ichigo o irete kudasai." The sentence can be translated as "Please place the raspberries in the barrel."

Library and Archives Canada Cataloguing in Publication

Bruins, David
   The legend of Ninja Cowboy Bear / written by David Bruins; illustrated by Hilary Leung.

ISBN 978-1-55453-486-9 (bound)

I. Leung, Hilary II. Title.

PS8603.R835L45 2009   jC813'.6   C2009-902225-7

www.ninja-cowboy-bear.com

FSC
Mixed Sources
Product group from well-managed forests, controlled sources and recycled wood or fibre
Cert no. DNV-COC-000025
www.fsc.org
© 1996 Forest Stewardship Council

Kids Can Press is a  Entertainment company